Kids Can Press gratefully acknowledges the financial support of the Government of Ontario, through the Ontario Media Development Corporation's Ontario Book Initiative; the Ontario Arts Council; the Canada Council for the Arts; and the Government of Canada, through the CBF, for our publishing activity.

Published in Canada and the U.S. by Kids Can Press Ltd.
25 Dockside Drive, Toronto, ON M5A 0B5

Kids Can Press is a Corus Entertainment Inc. company

www.kidscanpress.com

Edited by Debbie Rogosin
Designed by Marie Bartholomew
Illustrations by Serena Malyon

Printed and bound in Shenzhen, China, in 9/2016, by C & C Offset

CM 17 0 9 8 7 6 5 4 3 2 1

Library and Archives Canada Cataloguing in Publication

Dyer, Heather, 1970–, author
　　Magic in the city / written by Heather Dyer ; illustrated by Serena Malyon.

ISBN 978-1-77138-203-8 (hardback)

　　I. Malyon, Serena, illustrator II. Title.

PS8557.Y476M33 2017　　　jC813'.6　　　C2016-902615-9

Magic
in the City

WRITTEN BY
HEATHER DYER

ILLUSTRATIONS BY
SERENA MALYON

Kids Can Press

For Kate and Abbey — H.D.

CHAPTER 1

THE MAGICIAN

The magician was standing outside Coffee Central at the highway service stop. He was wearing a black top hat and a satin cloak, and he had a collection of curious-looking objects laid out on a rug. "Lovely oil lamp, this!" he cried, holding up what looked like a small brass watering can. "Still contains the genie!"

When none of the passersby took any notice, he said, "No? What about a white dove, then? Going cheap!" Reaching inside his cloak, he produced a dove as slim as a bar of soap. He tossed it into the air, and it flapped away to join several others on the roof of Coffee Central.

Simon Grubb stopped to watch. His mother stopped, too. And so, reluctantly, did Jake.

"Bonjour, madame," said the magician, tipping his hat to the boys' mother. "Philippe Fontaine. Pleased to meet you."

"Hello," said Rachel Grubb.

Philippe Fontaine stroked a long black box with stars along the side. "I don't suppose I can interest you in a box for sawing people in half?"

"We haven't got room in the car, unfortunately."

"Ah! On holiday, are we?"

"No," said Simon. "We're going to live in Dulwich with our auntie Helen. Our dad isn't coming with us because he's —"

"He's away," said Jake.

"I see," said the magician. His eyes were as blue as a husky dog's, and, strangely, it seemed as though he really *did* see. "In that case, what about a pair of white gloves? Or a top hat?"

"No thanks," said Jake, who was eleven. He had never much liked magicians. Or clowns. He didn't like men who flirted with his mother, either.

"Do you really saw people in half?" asked Simon, who was only six.

"Of course he doesn't," said Jake.

"As a matter of fact," said Philippe Fontaine, "I have sawn one hundred and twenty-nine ladies in half in this very box. Alas, I shall do it no longer."

"Why not?" said Simon.

"Nobody has time for magic nowadays." The magician gestured toward the people going past. "Busy-busy-busy, see? My only fans these days are children, and children don't have any cash."

"I've got cash!" Simon said.

"No, you don't," said Jake. Simon's coin collection was in his suitcase. It contained several American quarters, a one-franc piece and a penny that had been flattened by a train. Jake, on the other hand, had a £20 bill hidden in his sock for emergencies. But he wasn't about to mention it now.

The magician winked at Simon. "Keep your cash, young man," he said. From his pocket he produced a large black stopwatch. "You can have this for nothing."

"What does it do?" asked Simon.

"It stops time. And as for *you*," said the

magician, turning his light-blue eyes on Jake, "are you an armchair traveler?"

"What?"

"Do you want to visit far-off destinations but can't afford the airfare? Would you like to go straight from the brochure to the poolside at the click of a button?"

"No," said Jake. "Not re—"

"Well, now you can! The Magic Camera puts you in the picture." The magician picked up a camera on a long leather strap and handed it to Jake. It looked like the old-fashioned sort that you have to buy rolls of film for.

"That's very kind. What do you say, Jake?" said his mother.

"Thanks," muttered Jake.

"My pleasure," said Philippe Fontaine, turning away to attend to an old lady who was trying on a black top hat.

"Come on, boys," said their mother. "Aunt Helen's expecting us by seven."

They all went into Coffee Central. There was a long lineup. Just in front of them was a small boy wearing a satin cloak. In front of him was an old man shuffling a deck of cards; then two girls, each hugging a large white rabbit; and finally a small boy who kept whacking his mother's backside with a magic wand. It took ages to get served. Then Simon needed to use the washroom. By the time they came out, the magician was rolling up his carpet.

"You've sold it all?" said Simon, surprised.

"Everything but the carpet. I don't suppose you want it?"

"Oh, no," said their mother. "I don't think —"

"Yes!" cried Simon. "We do!"

So Philippe Fontaine gave the rolled-up carpet to the boys, who staggered under the weight of it.

"It's very obedient," said Philippe Fontaine. "It goes wherever you tell it. I'd keep it myself, but it doesn't like the wet."

"Why would it get wet?" said Jake.

"The sea, young man! I plan to sail the world aboard my yacht, the *Suzette*, charting the movements of the stars and writing online horoscopes." He tapped the side of his nose in a knowing way. "Astrology. It's the thing of the future."

Their mother laughed. "It certainly is! Good luck."

"The same to you. And don't forget — *keep that carpet dry!*"

***

Since their rental car was already crammed with suitcases, the only thing to do was to fold the carpet in half, lay it flat across the backseat and sit on it. It was mysteriously slippery, and as soon as the car pulled out, Simon slid across the backseat into Jake.

"Stay on your own side!" said Jake, giving him a shove.

"Ow!"

"Settle down, you two," said their mother, "or I'll give that carpet back."

But when they drove past Coffee Central, Philippe Fontaine had gone. Only the white doves remained. There were several pecking on the ground, and one perched on the roof.

CHAPTER 2

HANNAH

Hannah was standing at her bedroom window, looking out across the nighttime city. Aunt Rachel and the boys were supposed to have arrived at seven o'clock — but now it was nearly ten and they still hadn't turned up. "Do you think they're lost?" she said.

"I'm sure they'll find their way," said Hannah's mother, closing the curtains. "Now, *bed*!"

Hannah climbed into bed. "Do you think the boys will like living here?" she asked.

"I'm sure they'll get used to it," her mother said. "Of course, it's not an easy time for them."

"Why not?"

"Well, they didn't *want* to move. Jake and Simon will need to start new schools and make new friends. And they couldn't bring their dog with them. It means they won't see much of their father, either. Jake has taken it particularly hard, apparently."

"Why didn't they stay in Canada, then?"

"Rachel can't afford a big old house like that. Not on her own." Hannah's mother sighed. "I'm afraid your uncle John has rather left them in the lurch. No, it's best they stay with us until Aunt Rachel's on her feet again. Now get to sleep; you'll see them in the morning." She kissed Hannah goodnight, switched out the light and went downstairs.

For a long time Hannah lay with her eyes wide open in the dark.

She had last seen her cousins a year ago, at their house in Canada. She'd liked Aunt Rachel's house. It was surrounded by pine trees, and there was a rusty swing set and a sagging trampoline in the backyard. Sometimes, early in the morning, you could see deer at the edge of the forest. Inside the house there were lots of potted plants and dream catchers hanging in the windows.

Simon had only been five at the time. He was a scruffy, blond boy whose tongue was always the same color as the Popsicle he was sucking. Jake was older — a year older than Hannah. He liked building tree forts and drawing cartoons, and he'd let his hair grow long in front so that he had to flick it back if he wanted to look at you (which wasn't often). The boys spent most of their time in the woods, and everywhere they went, their old black Labrador, Monty, went with them.

"Rachel lets those boys run feral," Hannah heard her mother say.

Hannah wasn't exactly sure what "feral" meant, but she liked the sound of it. She'd tried keeping up with the boys, but she didn't have much experience bushwhacking or jumping from rock to rock across rushing rivers. And sandals aren't much good for crossing bogs. Sooner or later, the boys always came to a place where Hannah was unable to follow.

Once, while trying to find her way home alone, Hannah got lost. Eventually, she had stumbled out of the woods onto a logging road that led back to Aunt Rachel's house. But by the time she got home she was crying, covered in scratches, and was missing her hair ribbon. After that, Hannah had spent the rest of the week reading *The Lion, the Witch and the Wardrobe* on Aunt Rachel's porch.

This time would be different though. Aunt Rachel and the boys would be the visitors, and Hannah was looking forward to showing them around. She would take them to see the dinosaurs at the Natural History Museum, the treetop walkways at Kew Gardens, the changing of the guard at Buckingham Palace and —

The doorbell rang.

Hannah sat up to listen better. She heard her father say, "Jake? Simon? My word! Look how much you've grown."

"The traffic was appalling!" said Aunt Rachel. Then the voices retreated to the front room. But eventually, Hannah heard suitcases being dragged upstairs. "Sleep tight, boys. See you in the morning," said Aunt Rachel. Then the house was quiet.

But not entirely quiet. Hannah could make out the murmur of her cousins' voices in the room next door. A moment later there came a muffled shout and a *thud*. What were they doing in there? Hannah threw back her covers, slipped out of bed and tiptoed down the corridor.

***

Jake hated England. Everything here was tiny. The houses were all squashed tight together. The cars were small. The roads were narrow. Even Aunt Helen's refrigerator was half the size of theirs at home. He didn't see why they'd had to come here at all. Couldn't they have found someone in New Brunswick to stay with? He was pretty sure his aunt Helen didn't want them here, either. The house was full of little notices that said things like: DON'T FORGET TO FLUSH and PLEASE TAKE OFF YOUR SHOES. Their cousin Hannah was a drag, too. Last summer she'd gotten lost in the woods, and Jake had been blamed for leaving her behind. But it wasn't his fault if she kept following them and then wimping out and going home, was it?

Just then, Simon, who had been bouncing from bed to bed, landed with a crash on Philippe Fontaine's carpet, then sat down and began pulling off his shoes. "What do you think Dad is doing now?" he asked.

Jake glanced at his watch. "Having dinner, probably."

"On his own?"

"No. In the cafeteria." Jake preferred not to think about his father. The last time Jake had seen him, he had made Jake promise to take care of Simon and their mother. But how was he supposed to do that? Did his father think Jake could pay the mortgage with his paper route? Unless he won the lottery or robbed a bank, he didn't see how he could take care of anything.

Jake flopped into bed and thumbed through the *Pocket Guide to London* on the bedside table. There were pictures of Buckingham Palace, the London Eye and the waxworks in Madame Tussauds — none of which interested Jake. Then he came across a picture of a crown in a glass case. He paused. "*The Crown Jewels,*" said the book, "*feature some of the world's largest and most valuable gems. Several attempts have been made to steal the Crown Jewels from the Tower, most famously by Colonel Blood in 1671. But none have yet succeeded.*"

Jake looked at the crown thoughtfully.

"What are you reading?" asked Simon.

"A book about London," said Jake.

"Is there a picture of Buckingham Palace?" said Simon. "I want to meet the — *aah!*"

Jake glanced up. The carpet had risen off the floor and was undulating gently as though it was floating on water. Simon was still sitting on it.

Jake's mouth fell open, and the *Pocket Guide to London* slid to the floor with a thump.

"You see?" cried Simon. "I *told* you it was a magic carpet."

CHAPTER 3

THE MAGIC CARPET

There was a line of light beneath the boys'
bedroom door. Hannah knocked softly. There
was no answer. She knocked again a little more
loudly. "Jake?" she hissed.

Footsteps crossed the room, then the door
opened a crack and Jake looked out. He was taller
than Hannah remembered, and his dark hair fell
forward, over one eye. He was wearing a raincoat
and a T-shirt with the face of a wolf on it.

"Oh," said Jake. "It's you. What do you want?"

"I thought I heard a noise," said Hannah.

"What sort of noise?"

"I don't know. It sounded like —"

"*Jake!*" came a cry from inside the room.

"Was that Simon?" said Hannah.

"JAKE!" came the cry again.

Jake made an irritated noise. "Come in. Quick!" he said, and he pulled Hannah in and shut the door.

"What's going on?" said Hannah. "I … *Simon?*"

Simon was sitting cross-legged on an oriental rug, which was floating level with the windowsill. He was wearing his coat and backpack. "Hello!" he said, waving.

Hannah stared at him, speechless.

"It's a magic carpet," said Simon. "The magician gave it to us." He started telling Hannah all about Philippe Fontaine and his white doves and the long black box with stars along the side.

But Hannah wasn't listening. At the word "magic," a thrill had gone through her. "A magic carpet?" she whispered.

Jake opened the window. The night air blew into the room and made the curtains billow. He stepped onto the bed in his socks and climbed aboard the carpet. It sagged a little in the middle.

"What are you doing?" said Hannah, alarmed.

"We're going out," said Jake.

"Out? You can't go out! You're supposed to be in bed."

"Give us a push, will you?" said Jake. He drew the edges of the carpet up on either side and, reluctantly, Hannah helped him nudge it through the window. Once outside, Jake held on to the sill and offered his other hand to Hannah. "Coming?"

Hannah hesitated. Ever since watching *Aladdin*, she had longed to ride a magic carpet. Once, she had even sat cross-legged on the oriental rug in the hall and commanded it to take her to the Taj Mahal in India. But nothing had happened. Now she had her chance — but the gap between the carpet and the windowsill was just the wrong distance. Hannah could see the flagstone path below. It was a long way to fall.

"Where are you going?" she asked.

"The Tower of London," said Simon.

As soon as the words were out of his mouth the carpet began moving off. Jake was forced to let go of the windowsill, and by the time he'd recovered his balance, the carpet was already halfway over the garden next door.

"Wait!" called Hannah. "Come back!"

But it was too late. The carpet was rising steadily. Up it went, across the rooftops and away. Soon Jake and Simon were just two dark figures aboard a small dark square. Then they were gone.

Hannah waited for a long time, but the boys did not return. Once again, they had left her

behind. Oh! If only she'd been braver. She was
reminded of the time she'd lost her nerve on
the high diving board at last year's swimming
extravaganza and had had to climb back down the
ladder with everyone watching.

Hannah shivered. It was chilly standing by the
open window, and her teeth began to chatter.
Where *were* the boys? Surely they should have
come back by now. Had one of them fallen off?
Or had the carpet kept on flying straight across
London and out to sea? How long had they been
gone, anyway? She reached for what looked like a
digital alarm clock on the bedside table. It was a
strange sort of clock, though. On the front it said
TIME IS MOTION and there was one button to
press. "Time is motion?" murmured Hannah. She
pressed the button. Immediately, she felt a strange
popping in her ears, and the numbers on the
digital display began counting down. So it wasn't a
clock after all; it was a stopwatch. Hannah pressed
the button a few more times, but the numbers
kept on going, so she put it back and looked out
across the silent city. It was unusually quiet, as

though the whole of London was asleep. The carpet was nowhere in sight.

Hannah knew then what she must do. She must go and tell her parents what had happened. They would call the police, and a helicopter would be dispatched to find the boys and bring them home safely. Hannah left the window open in case the boys returned, and went to her parents' room. She knocked softly. There was no answer, so she crept in and stood beside the bed. Her parents were both lying perfectly still. "Mum?" she whispered.

Her mother didn't move.

Hannah reached out to touch her mother's shoulder, then hesitated. If the boys didn't *need* rescuing, they'd be furious with her for telling. Her parents would confiscate the carpet when the boys returned, and then Hannah would never get to ride it. Perhaps she should wait a little bit longer before she raised the alarm?

Hannah tiptoed back to her room and got into bed. Her feet were freezing. She curled up, shivering, and wondered what the boys were doing. She didn't know why they had wanted to go to the Tower of London. If it had been up to her, she'd have chosen somewhere much more exciting, somewhere like the great white roof of Millennium Dome. It might be fun to land on it and walk about a bit; she'd always wondered if it was bouncy, like a trampoline. Or maybe she would go all the way to North America and hover in the mist above Niagara Falls, or fly through the Grand Canyon.

Hannah lay awake, listening for the boys' return. But the house was so quiet that eventually she fell asleep. While the stopwatch counted down in the room next door, Hannah dreamed that she was sitting cross-legged on the magic carpet, wearing baggy harem trousers and pointy silver slippers. By the time the stopwatch had reached zero, Hannah was sailing high above the sleeping town of Agra, with the distant spires of the Taj Mahal pinkish in the sunrise.

CHAPTER 4

LONDON AT NIGHT

The boys flew on, high above the city. It was a cool, clear night, and far below the lights of London glittered.

"What's that?" asked Simon, pointing to a dark pathway winding through the lights.

"It must be the River Thames," said Jake.

As soon as he said "Thames," the carpet started dropping. Soon they could see roads streaming with traffic and office buildings all lit up like cages of light. Down and down went the carpet, straight toward the glittering black water of the River Thames. For one awful

moment it seemed as though it was going to
skid to a stop on the surface like a giant swan.
But the carpet seemed to know better. It flew
on, upriver, low enough that Simon could trail
his fingers in the water.

The carpet passed a tour boat called *The
Pride of London*, with lots of people on board,
all drinking champagne. Simon stood up and
waved. "Hi!" he yelled.

"Sit down!" snapped Jake.

A little farther on, the carpet passed beneath
a bridge, sending a flock of roosting pigeons
flapping out from underneath. And when they
rounded the next bend they could see a huge
building on the bank of the Thames, with
dozens of spires and four Union Jacks flying.

Jake unzipped Simon's backpack and got out
the *Pocket Guide to London*. "That's the Palace of
Westminster," he said, consulting the guidebook,
"and Big Ben."

Obediently, the carpet left the river and headed
north, but just as they were approaching Big Ben's
huge clock face, Simon shouted, "LOOK! The

London Eye!" So the carpet swung east and flew so close to the giant Ferris wheel that they could see tourists riding in the capsules. Jake and Simon waved, and the tourists crowded against the glass to take photographs.

"Where next?" said Jake.

"Buckingham Palace!" said Simon, and the carpet flew straight up the tree-lined Mall and circled the palace so closely that the boys could see people drawing the curtains in upstairs rooms.

It can go to your head, being above everyone else. Jake started flicking through the guidebook shouting out landmarks: "Hyde Park! Kensington Palace! Trafalgar Square! Regent's Park Mosque!"

The carpet flew back and forth across the twinkling city. They passed through Euston Station and heard the train announcements. They circled the dome of St. Paul's Cathedral, and they flew low over Piccadilly Circus, calling down to people in the streets.

But eventually, far away above the city skyline, the night sky began to pale. One by one the streetlights went out. The twinkle of the night was giving way to the cold light of dawn. When they passed Big Ben for the second time, it was chiming five o'clock in the morning.

"We'd better get to the Tower," said Jake, "before it opens for the day."

The carpet turned and headed east.

"I'm tired," said Simon, yawning. "Let's go home."

At the word "home," the carpet did a U-turn.

"Not till we've been to the Tower," said Jake.

The carpet turned around again.

"Home!" said Simon.

"The Tower!"

"Home!"

"THE TOWER!"

The carpet swung first to the left and then to the right, confused, until the boys began to get dizzy.

"Cut it out!" yelled Jake.

"But it's starting to rain," said Simon. "The carpet doesn't like the wet."

Jake looked up. Sure enough, storm clouds were gathering. Then he felt a speck of rain upon his eyelid. "All right! Home," he said.

The carpet turned around again. But it was flying into the wind now, and it moved slowly, as though it was a struggle. And the wind was getting stronger. The carpet began to get buffeted left and right, and soon the boys had to hold on to the edges to avoid being thrown off. A moment later there was a low rumble overhead, and then the rain began in earnest.

"Up! *Up!*" yelled Jake.

The carpet started rising. Higher and higher it went until it was up inside the clouds, and for a while the boys could see nothing but rushing mist. Then the carpet shot out above the mist, and the boys found themselves blinking in bright sunshine. The sky was an endless blue and the clouds were spread out below them like a vast white duvet.

Simon put his hood back. "Is this heaven?"

"Nope," said Jake. "It's the troposphere. What people don't realize is that it's *always* sunny above the clouds." He rummaged in Simon's backpack and took out a bag of cheese and onion chips, half an egg-and-cress sandwich and a chunk of fruitcake wrapped in foil. It was the remains of the packed lunch from the day before and was a strange sort of breakfast, but after riding a magic carpet all night it was just what they wanted. "Cake?" said Jake.

"Yes, please," said Simon.

The carpet floated on. It was peaceful above the clouds, and very quiet. "The best place to be in a storm," said Jake, opening the bag of chips, "is *above* it. It's because of the turbulence."

"Turbulence?" said Simon, through a mouthful of cake.

"Rough air," explained Jake. "In fact, aircraft

often fly at this altitude because there's less risk
of —"

From out of nowhere came an airplane. The
boys barely had time to glimpse a row of little
round windows, each containing one astonished
face, before the carpet was tossed aside in a roar
of hot air. "Hang on!" screamed Jake.

The chips went fluttering to the winds like
autumn leaves. The fruitcake and the sandwich
were flung in opposite directions. Round and
down the carpet went, through the swirling mist,
and when it finally stopped spinning it was back
below the clouds again. It was still raining.

"Up! Up!" yelled Jake. The carpet rose briefly
but sank again, as though the effort was too great.

"We're sinking," said Simon.

Jake seized a corner of the carpet and tried
to wring it out. But it was no use. The carpet
was waterlogged. Down, down, down they went,
toward the waking city. Soon they could hear the
clang of recycling trucks and the roar of traffic.
The day had begun, and the carpet was heading
straight into the rush hour.

CHAPTER 5

THE UNIDENTIFIED FLYING OBJECT

When Hannah woke up, the clock on her bedside table said 8:55 a.m. Downstairs she could hear voices and the clatter of dishes. She had fallen asleep! She jumped out of bed, put on her fluffy pink robe and monster-feet slippers and went and knocked on the boys' bedroom door. There was no answer, so she opened the door a crack and went in. The beds were empty, and the window was still open exactly as she'd left it. Where were the boys? Were they still out there somewhere on the magic carpet? Or were they in the kitchen, eating breakfast?

Alarmed, Hannah hurried downstairs. Only her father and Aunt Rachel were at the table. They were eating toast and marmalade and watching the nine o'clock news.

"Hello, sweetheart!" said Aunt Rachel.

"Hello," said Hannah. Her aunt was wearing a floral kimono, and her long, wavy hair was pinned up with butterfly clips. Not for the first time, Hannah thought how strange it was that Aunt Rachel and her mother were sisters. They were so different.

"Come and sit by me," said her aunt, "and tell me everything. What have you been doing?"

"Nothing!" said Hannah guiltily. "I mean, nothing much."

Hannah's mother came over then, with the coffee pot. "You've had a nice long lie-in," she remarked. "Did you sleep all right?"

"Yes, thanks," said Hannah.

"Any sign of Jake and Simon?"

Hannah stared at her mother. "What?"

"Jake and Simon. Are they awake?"

"I don't know," said Hannah truthfully.

"Perhaps I ought to go and wake them."

"*No!*" cried Hannah. "You shouldn't wake people up when they're on holiday."

"Well, all right. I'll give them a little bit longer."

Hannah sat down and began tapping the top of her boiled egg with the back of her spoon. Normally, she enjoyed a boiled egg, but today her mind was elsewhere. Where were her cousins? Had they been blown off course and out to sea? Were they stranded on a rooftop? Or lost? What if one of them had fallen off the carpet and was lying in some alley with his head cracked open and his brains spilled out like Humpty Dumpty's … Ugh!

Hannah pushed her egg aside. She should have woken her parents last night. If something terrible had happened to the boys, Aunt Rachel would never forgive her. Nobody would. You could probably get sent to prison for keeping a secret like that — and the longer she kept it, the worse things would get. She had no choice. She would have to confess.

"Dad," said Hannah. "I need to tell you something. Last night I —"

"Shhh!" said her father. "Listen to this!" He turned up the volume on the television.

"— *completely gridlocked*," said the announcer, "*after sightings of an unidentified flying object.*"

"A what?" said Aunt Rachel.

"*At seven thirty the aircraft was seen flying at low altitude down Kensington High Street. Eyewitnesses report that there were at least two individuals on board. The following footage was posted on YouTube by a member of the public.*"

The picture changed then, and at first it wasn't clear what was happening. People were shouting and running and pointing at something in the sky. Then there it was: the carpet! The picture was too blurry to make out much, but it was clear that there were two figures aboard. They both had their hoods up, and one was wearing a backpack. The carpet veered left and disappeared between two buildings.

"The Civil Aviation Authority," said the announcer, *"says there is no reason to think that the aircraft presents a danger to the public. However, drivers are being asked to avoid the city center unless absolutely necessary."*

Then the next news item came up: a donkey rescued from a well. Hannah's father switched off the television.

"Good grief," said Aunt Rachel. "What do you think it is?"

"Some sort of hoax, no doubt," said Hannah's father. He glanced at his watch. "I thought we could take the boys to the Natural History Museum this morning. What do you think?"

Aunt Rachel stood up. "I'll go and wake them."

"No, no. Finish your toast," said Hannah's father. "I'll go." And before Hannah could stop him, he had pushed back his chair and was heading for the door.

CHAPTER 6

GROUNDED

Jake and Simon were flying down Clapham High Street, level with the upstairs windows. Vehicles pulled over, and people got out of their cars to take pictures of the carpet as it flew past. In the distance, the boys could hear the wail of sirens.

"Nelsons Row!" yelled Jake, squinting at the street signs through the rain. Immediately, the carpet swung left, down a quiet residential road.

"Triangle Place!"

The carpet turned right.

"Park Hill!"

"West Road!"

The carpet zigzagged left and right, taking corners so tightly that the boys had to cling to the edges to avoid being thrown off. Then, at the end of Kings Avenue, the carpet reached a busy intersection. Cars honked and swerved.

"Dulwich!" screamed Jake.

The carpet took a sharp left and joined the flow of traffic on the South Circular. It flew straight over a pedestrian crossing, causing several schoolchildren to jump back in alarm. For a while it tailed a van with a barking dog in the back. Then the turbulence from a passing truck nudged the carpet off the road altogether. And all the while the carpet was sinking. Soon it was barely skimming the sidewalk. In a moment it would touch down.

There was only one thing for it.

"Jump!" said Jake. He and Simon got to their feet and stood like surfers, with their knees bent and their arms held out for balance. "One … two … *ugh*!"

Jake fell flat on his face, but Simon landed lightly and kept on running. He caught up with the carpet and put his foot on it. "Now what do we do?" he said.

"Walk," said Jake.

So they rolled up the carpet and set off, carrying it between them. But carpets are heavy when they're wet, and saggy in the middle, and it was raining even harder now. On they trudged, left-right, left-right through the rain, with the traffic zipping past. Eventually, Jake dropped his end of the carpet. "Stop a second," he said. "I'm going to flag somebody down."

Simon looked uncertain. "Mum said if we get lost we should stay where we are until she comes to find us."

"That was in Value Foods. How will she find us here?"

Simon unrolled the carpet on the grass, sat down and opened his backpack while Jake stood at the roadside and waved his arms. Several cars honked, and a school bus went past full of waving children. But nobody stopped.

Eventually, Jake returned to the carpet and sat down, disgusted. He glanced at his watch. It was ten past nine. Sooner or later, their mother would go upstairs to wake them. She would discover that their beds were empty. Aunt Helen or Uncle Robert would call the police. A search party would be sent out, and everything would be Jake's fault, just like it always was.

Gloomily, Jake watched the passing cars. It was hard to believe that just half an hour ago they'd been flying across London shouting down to people in the streets. Now here they were, grounded, with everybody passing them by. It was just like life, thought Jake. One day you had your own bedroom and friends and a dad who took you fishing. The next day you had nothing. Oh, *why* hadn't they gone to the Tower of London first, instead of wasting the night flying around London?

From his backpack, Simon produced a damp apple speckled with crumbs. "Want some?" he asked.

"No," said Jake.

Simon polished the apple on his coat and took a loud bite. Jake glared at him.

"What?" said Simon.

"Nothing."

Simon crunched his apple. "Oh, well," he said. "It could be worse."

"How?"

"At least we didn't get arrested by the ..." Simon's voice trailed off. A police car had just pulled up beside them with its blue lights flashing. The door opened, and a police officer got out. He came over and stood with his hands on his hips, looking down at them. "Well, well, well," he said. "What's going on here?"

"We're having a picnic," said Jake.

"A picnic? This is no place for a picnic, boys."

"We were just leaving," said Jake. "Come on, Simon."

"Not so fast," said the police officer. "Where are your shoes?"

"At home."

"Where's home?"

"Dulwich."

The police officer frowned. "You're telling me you walked all the way from Dulwich in your socks?"

"No," said Simon. "We flew."

"There's no need to be smart, son. And *you*," said the officer to Jake, "are old enough to know better. Now get in the car, both of you. You can put your rug in the back."

There was no point in arguing. The boys rolled up the waterlogged carpet and put it in the trunk. Then they got into the police car, and it pulled away to join the traffic on the South Circular.

CHAPTER 7

HOME AGAIN

Hannah's father came downstairs looking puzzled. "They aren't here," he said. "They've gone."

"Gone?" said Hannah's mother. "Don't be silly. Did you check the bathroom?"

"Yes. They aren't in the front room, either. Or the garden. They aren't anywhere."

Hannah's heart thumped. She would have to tell her parents everything. But just as she opened her mouth, the doorbell rang.

"Perhaps that's them," said her father.

They all went hopefully down the hall, but when they opened the door they found a solemn-looking police officer on the step.

"Mrs. Grubb?" he said. "Are these two yours?"
And out from behind him stepped Jake and
Simon.

"Jake! Simon!" said Aunt Rachel. "Where have
you been?"

"I found them on the South Circular," said the
officer, "having a picnic."

"A picnic!"

"Look at you! You're soaking wet," said
Hannah's mother. "And where are your shoes?"

"We didn't think we'd be walking far," said
Jake, stiffly.

At least they were safe, thought Hannah. But where was the carpet? She glanced down the path. There was no sign of it. Had they lost it? Or had it been taken from them?

"Go on in, then, boys," said the officer, "before you catch a cold."

Simon ran straight upstairs with his backpack bouncing. Jake stomped up wearily in his soggy socks.

"We're very grateful, officer," Aunt Rachel said. "We're not from here, you see. We're visiting. Please come in and have a cup of tea."

"Thank you," said the police officer, "but I can't stop. We've got our hands full this morning. You'll have heard about the UFO, I take it?"

"Yes!" said Hannah's father. "What do you think it is?"

"Some sort of hoax. Couple of kids, probably."

"Well, I hope you find them, officer."

"Oh, we will," said the police officer, and off he went.

"A *picnic*?" said Hannah's father, in disbelief.

"You don't think they were running away, do you, Rachel?" said Hannah's mother.

"No, no!" said Aunt Rachel, shocked. "They were probably just exploring."

"Exploring? This is London, Rachel! They can't just go exploring whenever they like. Anything could have happened."

Aunt Rachel sighed. "I know, I know. I'll have a word with them."

They went back toward the kitchen, talking. Hannah waited until they had gone, then she ran upstairs to the boys' room and burst in without knocking. "Where is it?" she demanded.

"Where's what?" said Jake. He was hopping on one foot, trying to extricate the other from his wet jeans.

"The carpet!"

"Oh — that. It's outside."

Hannah went to the window. Sure enough, there was the carpet. It was rolled up against the wall, beside the garbage cans.

"You can't leave it there," said Hannah. "What if someone takes it?"

"No one will take it," said Jake. "It's soaking wet."

"You got it wet?" cried Hannah.

"It rained," explained Simon. "That's why it won't fly anymore."

"You mean it's *ruined*?"

"It wasn't intentional," said Jake, climbing into bed.

All of a sudden Hannah felt like crying. Ever since she'd woken up, she'd been imagining that the boys had either been drowned at sea or were lying on the ground somewhere with their heads smashed open. Now here they were, without a scratch on them. It hadn't occurred to them to apologize for leaving her behind, or to thank her for keeping their secret — and to top it off, they'd ruined the carpet! She yanked Jake's duvet. "Get up! We've got to bring it in and dry it out."

Jake snatched his duvet back. "We'll bring it in later."

"Later will be too late."

"Well, we can't bring it in now, can we?" said Jake.

"Why not?"

"For starters, your mother will see."

"See what?" said a familiar voice, and they all looked around to see Hannah's mother standing in the doorway.

"You'll see how tired we are," said Jake. "It must be jet lag."

"The cure for jet lag," said Hannah's mother firmly, "is to adapt to the local time zone as soon as possible. Get up, come downstairs and have some breakfast. Hannah, let's leave the boys to get dressed, shall we?"

Hannah shot Jake a dark look, then followed her mother downstairs.

***

Absently, Hannah resumed tapping the top of her boiled egg with the back of her spoon. Perhaps the damage to the carpet wasn't permanent. Perhaps, once she'd dried it with her hair dryer, it would be all right again. But first they would have to get the carpet upstairs without her mother noticing.

"Are you going to eat that egg, Hannah?" said her mother sharply, "or just keep tapping it?"

Hannah put down her spoon and began picking off the shell. If they *did* get the carpet flying again, just imagine where they could go! She could see herself flying over the Alps wearing her woolly hat and winter coat. Or skimming the treetops of the Amazon forest at dusk. Or crossing the Sahara desert at dawn. Or —

Just then, Jake and Simon came thundering down the stairs.

"Ah. Here you are," said Hannah's mother. "Would you like a boiled egg, boys?"

"Yes, please," said the boys.

To Hannah's astonishment, her cousins no longer looked tired or wet. They ate their boiled eggs, and then Simon downed a glass of orange juice and started tucking into a bowl of cornflakes. Jake ate two pieces of toast with butter and jam and then asked Hannah's mother if she had any granola. And all the while he was bombarding Hannah's father with questions like,

"Where's the Bank of England?" and "How much are the Crown Jewels worth?"

"Jake! Let your uncle read his paper," said Aunt Rachel.

"I don't mind," said Hannah's father, who was happy to answer all of Jake's questions at length. "It's good to see a thirst for knowledge."

Hannah frowned. Jake was up to something, she was sure of it. But what?

As soon as they had finished eating, Jake and Simon ran back upstairs.

Quickly, Hannah scooped up the last few spoonfuls of egg, then pushed back her chair and went after them.

"Tell the boys we're leaving in five minutes, would you?" her mother called.

But Hannah had already gone.

CHAPTER 8

THE STOPWATCH

Hannah found the boys sitting on the floor of their room with a collection of maps and guidebooks lying open between them. They had their coats on, and Jake had a large camera hanging from a strap around his neck.

"We're leaving in five minutes," Hannah informed them. "We have to bring the carpet in before we go."

Jake waved his hand dismissively. "Relax," he said. "There's plenty of time."

"No, there isn't!"

"Yes, there is," said Simon, grinning. "We've

got all the time we want, now that we've got *this*." He showed her the stopwatch. "It stops time. Philippe Fontaine gave it to me."

Hannah stared at the stopwatch. It was the one she'd found in the boys' room while they were out on the carpet. "You can't stop *time*," she said, uncertainly.

"Actually, you can," said Jake. "We just did."

"When?"

"Just now. We went downstairs and got some orange juice. Then we came upstairs again and had a nap."

"I didn't see you," said Hannah.

"That's because you were stopped," said Jake.

Hannah frowned. She had pressed the button last night, but nothing had stopped then. Or had it? Her parents *had* been sleeping very soundly.

"Hold on to my sleeve," said Simon, "and I'll show you."

"Show me later," said Hannah. "There isn't time now."

As if to prove it, they all heard Hannah's mother shouting, "Ready, boys?"

"Coming!" said Jake. But he made no move to go downstairs. Instead, he linked his arm in Simon's. "Well?" he said to Hannah. "Are you coming, or not?"

"No!"

"Suit yourself. Ready, Simon?" said Jake.

"Ready," said Simon.

"No. Wait!" Hannah reached out to stop him, but just as she touched Simon's sleeve, he said, "Time is motion," and pressed the button on the stopwatch.

Instantly, everything was muffled. It was like when you put your head under water or put your fingers in your ears. "What happened?" said Hannah. Her voice sounded strange, and she waggled her jaw to make her ears pop.

"Time has stopped," said Jake.

Hannah went to the window. Her father was standing beside the car. She opened the window and leaned out. "Dad?" she shouted. Her father didn't move. Nothing did. The traffic had stopped. Mrs. Miles from next door had paused in the middle of hanging out her washing. Even the clouds were stationary. It was as though the whole world was just a stage set.

"It's all right," said Simon. "It all comes back when the stopwatch gets to zero."

But Hannah had already rushed downstairs. She stopped in the kitchen doorway. Her mother had paused in the middle of making egg-and-cress sandwiches, like a clockwork toy whose batteries had died.

"Mum?" said Hannah. Her mother didn't turn around. Hannah crept closer and tugged her mother's sleeve. "*Mum!*"

Slowly, her mother began to topple. If it hadn't been for the boys rushing in just then, she might have crashed to the floor. But just in time, Jake caught her and set her upright.

Furiously, Hannah turned on him. "Bring her back again!"

"We can't," said Jake.

"Not until the numbers get to zero."

"When will that be?"

"Not long," said Jake. "We'll be back before they even notice that we've gone."

"Gone? Where are you going?"

"To the Bank of England," said Simon.

"The Bank of England!" cried Hannah. "What are you going there for?"

But Jake was already heading to the door.

"Wait! You can't leave me here on my own! Anything could happen."

"Nothing will happen," said Jake. "When the stopwatch gets to zero, everything will start up again, just like before."

"What am I supposed to do till then?"

"I don't know. Read a book or something."

They both went out. Hannah heard the front door bang behind them. Then silence. She studied her mother's unresponsive face. There was something unnerving about being alone with someone who was neither awake nor asleep. Hannah stood for a moment, dithering. Then she shouted, "Wait for me!" and hurried out after her cousins.

CHAPTER 9

THE SILENT CITY

Jake and Simon had already wheeled the bicycles out of the garage and were cycling down the street. Jake was on Hannah's father's mountain bike, and Simon was flying along behind him on Hannah's old pink bike with training wheels. The boys rounded the bend and disappeared.

Still wearing her pink robe and monster-feet slippers, Hannah hurried to the garage, got out her own bike and, forgetting all about the magic carpet, pedaled after the others. She caught up with them at the end of the street, and they cycled on in close formation.

The world was still and silent, like early on a Sunday morning when everyone is still asleep. Nobody spoke. The only sound was the whir of their tires on the asphalt and the flutter of the little pink windmill on Simon's handlebars.

Hannah glanced up at the windows of the houses on either side. Had the people inside all just ground to a halt in the middle of talking on the phone or having a shower or making a cup of tea? And what about the people in the banks and the restaurants and the factories? Was everybody motionless? What about the gorillas in the zoo? The fish in the sea? The boats and the trains and the airplanes? Was it possible that *everything* had stopped?

They overtook a woman sitting on a motionless bike, and two small boys on scooters, both with one leg poised behind them, mid-kick. They cycled across busy intersections, through red lights and in and out of stationary traffic. The closer they got to the center of London, the more crowded the streets became. Soon the sidewalks were full of people who had all paused in mid-stride: business people with briefcases, parents with strollers,

schoolchildren crossing the road. Hannah stopped
her bike to stroke a fat Dalmatian on a leash,
but it felt hard and cold, like stroking a sofa,
and Hannah quickly drew her hand away. They
passed a sidewalk café full of people holding cups
of coffee and forkfuls of cake halfway to their
mouths. And then they came to a jewelry store
with a display of watches in the window.

Jake braked.

"What are we stopping here for?" said
Hannah. "I thought you wanted to see the Bank
of England?"

"Wait here," said Jake. "I won't be long." He
laid his bike on the sidewalk and went into the
shop. The door banged shut behind him.

Hannah looked at Simon anxiously. "What's he
up to?"

Simon shrugged.

"I'd better go and get him," said Hannah.

"I'll come, too," said Simon.

So they laid their bikes next to Jake's and went
inside. They found him peering into a glass case
displaying necklaces and rings. There was no one

else in the store except for an old man in a purple tie standing like a mannequin behind the counter.

"I told you to wait outside," said Jake, annoyed.

"Why? What are you doing?" said Hannah.

"Just looking," said Jake. He tried the door of the display case, but it was locked. "It's not fair," he said. "All those necklaces, just sitting there. I bet each one of them costs more than a house. If I could only —"

Then it happened. There was a blast of air, like when you're waiting at the station and an express train rushes through, then all the sounds were back. A voice behind them said, "Can I help you?" and they turned to see the old man with the purple tie smiling at them.

"No thanks," said Hannah, flushing.

"Take your time," said the man. "If you need anything, let me know."

"We were just leaving," said Hannah. She took Jake's sleeve and pulled him outside. Time was marching on again, and so were the pedestrians. But where they had left their bikes, a crowd had gathered. "Oh, *no!*" said Hannah.

An old woman was being helped up off the ground. She had dropped her bag of groceries, and potatoes were rolling in all directions. "I didn't even *see* those bikes!" she was saying. "They just *appeared*."

A man in a suit was sitting on the sidewalk with his trouser leg rolled up. He was dabbing at his knee with a tissue. "Are these your bikes?" he said. "They're a safety hazard."

"I'm so sorry," said Hannah. Her face was scarlet.

"You can't just leave them wherever you want, you know," said someone else. "People could get hurt."

"People *have* been hurt!" said the man.

The children helped the old woman retrieve her groceries, and she hobbled away. The business person rolled his trouser leg back down, glared at them and limped off. One by one the bystanders departed, and soon the sidewalk was a river of faces once again.

"We need more time," said Jake. "Simon, where's the stopwatch?"

"We can't do it here," protested Hannah. "Everyone will see."

"No, they won't," said Jake. "Look."

Hannah saw that he was right. The passersby were looking straight ahead, thinking only of their destinations.

"Ready?" said Jake.

"Ready," said Simon.

Just in time, Hannah grabbed Simon's arm.

"Time is motion!" said Simon, and pressed the button.

Instantly, the world stopped. The pedestrians were now as lifeless as an army of waxworks from Madame Tussauds.

"Let's go," said Jake.

"Don't you think it's time we were getting home?" said Hannah.

But Jake had already mounted his bike and was pedaling away. Hannah hesitated. She had noticed a stray potato on the ground. Not knowing what else to do, she picked it up and put it in the pocket of her robe. Then she got on her bike and cycled after the others.

CHAPTER 10

BUCKINGHAM PALACE

They crossed Vauxhall Bridge, weaving in and out of stationary vehicles, and went down Vauxhall Bridge Road and along Spur Road. And then there it was, right in front of them: Buckingham Palace. It looked just like it did on the postcards. The palace guards were standing at attention in their red tunics and bearskin hats, and the Royal Standard on the roof was as stiff as the flag on a sandcastle.

"She's home!" said Simon, braking.

"Who is?" said Hannah.

"The queen. That's the Royal Standard. It

means she's here." Simon dismounted and leaned his bike against the gold-tipped railings.

"What are you doing?" said Jake. "We're supposed to be going to the Bank of England."

"We can go there later," said Simon. "I want to meet the queen."

"Forget it," said Jake. "We haven't time."

"Yes, we do!" said Simon. "We've got all the time we want now. You said so yourself."

"But even if she *is* home," said Hannah, "you'll never find her. Do you know how many rooms there are in there?"

"Seven hundred and seventy-five," said Simon, pushing open the enormous wrought-iron gates.

"Hey!" said Jake. "Wait up! I don't want you wandering off. You've got the stopwatch, remember?"

But Simon was already heading across the forecourt. Jake made an exasperated sound. He turned to Hannah. "Wait here," he said. "We won't be long."

"I'm not waiting on my own!" said Hannah.

So they leaned their bikes against the railings and set off after Simon.

The windows of the palace seemed to watch them approach. But the palace guard stared ahead, unseeing, as they passed, and the sentries in their boxes remained as stiff as the figures in a cuckoo clock. The children walked straight up the steps, through the Grand Entrance and into a foyer with a domed ceiling so high and so ornate that when you looked up, it felt as if angels might start singing.

Simon ran up a wide, red-carpeted stairway and disappeared. Jake followed him.

"Do you even know where you're going?" cried Hannah.

The boys ignored her.

Hannah noticed a carousel displaying leaflets and brochures. So she helped herself to a map of the palace and put it in her pocket. Then she hurried after the others.

At the top of the stairs was an enormous room where everything was white and gold. There were huge mirrors with fancy gold frames, gold-upholstered chairs with legs carved into lion's feet, and crystal chandeliers cascading from the ceiling. Jake tried to lift a golden candlestick, but it was too heavy.

"I don't think we should touch anything," said Hannah nervously.

Together, they wandered through one grand room after another: rooms with yellow satin couches long enough to seat ten people and huge porcelain vases big enough to climb inside. Now Hannah knew how Belle must have felt when she entered the Beast's castle without knocking. Once, out of the corner of her eye, she glimpsed a movement on the far side of the room and saw a timid-looking girl staring back at her. "Oh!" she said. "I'm sorry! We just —" Then she realized she was speaking to her own reflection in a mirror.

"Who are you talking to?" said Jake.

"Nobody!" said Hannah, flushing.

They went through the Blue Drawing Room and the Green Drawing Room and the White Drawing Room, and presently they came to the Throne Room. It was empty except for two

red-velvet thrones positioned side by side on a
raised platform at the far end of the room, with a
red-velvet curtain on the wall behind them. Simon
immediately went investigating behind the velvet
curtain. Jake sat on one of the thrones. Despite
his runners and the camera hanging around his
neck, Jake looked surprisingly regal with his hands
resting on the throne's upholstered arms. After
a moment's hesitation, Hannah sat down on the
other one. It gave her a funny feeling, sitting up
there looking out across such a grand room. It
was like being on stage.

"Do you think she likes being queen?" said Hannah.

"Of course she likes it," said Jake. "She's rich, isn't she?"

"Just because she's rich," said Hannah, "it doesn't mean she's happy. Money isn't everything, you know."

"It is if you don't have any."

"It must be hard work, though. Don't you think?"

"Cutting ribbons and waving? That's not work." Jake gestured angrily at the room around them. "Why should one person have all *this*," he said, "when others don't even have *one* house of their own? And this isn't her only home, you know. There's Clarence House and Sandringham and Windsor Castle and Balmoral and …" He paused. "Where's Simon?"

"I don't know," said Hannah, looking around. "He was here a minute ago."

"Simon?" said Jake. He got down off his throne and pulled back the red curtain. Behind it was a door marked PRIVATE. The door was ajar, revealing a red-carpeted staircase.

"SIMON?" yelled Jake.

There was no reply, but a door banged faintly somewhere far away.

"I knew it!" said Jake. "I *knew* he'd do something like this."

They ran up the stairs and along a red-carpeted corridor calling, "Simon? Simon!" But there was no answer. Jake tried several doors, but most of them were locked, and those that weren't opened into storerooms or linen cupboards. There was no sign of Simon.

"Let's go back to the Throne Room," said Hannah. "Maybe he's waiting for us there."

Jake glanced at his watch. "We haven't time. We'll have to leave without him."

"We can't do that!" said Hannah. "Anyway, we've got all the time we want. We've got the stopwatch. Remember?"

"No, we don't," said Jake. "*Simon* has the stopwatch. Remember?"

Hannah looked at Jake in horror. He was right. As soon as the stopwatch got to zero, time would start again, and they would be caught trespassing in Buckingham Palace! "Quick," she said, turning on her heel. "Let's get out of here."

But it was too late. The moment the words were out of her mouth, she felt a popping in her ears and all the sounds were back again: the gurgle of the central heating, the drone of distant traffic and the murmur of voices from behind closed doors. Then, around the corner came a butler carrying a silver teapot on a silver tray. He stopped short when he saw them. "Hello," he said. "And who are you?"

For a moment, Hannah and Jake just stared at him. Then Jake yelled, "*Run!*"

CHAPTER 11

SIMON AND THE QUEEN

Later, Hannah realized that if they had simply apologized and explained that they were looking for Simon, the butler might even have helped them. But they didn't stop to think. They ran. Back along the corridor they went and down another flight of stairs, taking them two at a time. When they got to the bottom, they burst through double doors into a busy kitchen full of cooks in tall white hats.

"Hey! Out of my kitchen!" yelled the head chef.

Hannah and Jake dodged this way and that, ducking trays and hot plates. There was a crash as one chef dropped a platter of profiteroles, which scattered over the floor.

"Sorry!" cried Hannah.

The children charged through another set of doors into a room where lots of well-dressed people were having brunch. Diners paused with their forks halfway to their mouths as Hannah and Jake rushed past with several chefs in pursuit.

"Stop right there!" yelled a waiter.

The children ran through a door marked EXIT, up three flights of stairs and along yet another red-carpeted corridor. Jake tried the handles of several doors, but they were all locked. Then, at last, one opened. They rushed inside and slammed it shut behind them — and not a second too soon. The stampede of running feet and raised voices came barreling along the corridor, went straight past and disappeared. Somewhere, an alarm had started ringing.

Hannah and Jake looked around. They were in a small room lined with bookshelves. There was a leather sofa in front of a fireplace and an oil painting above the mantel. Hannah ran to the window. To her dismay, she saw that the palace guard had surrounded the Grand Entrance, bayonets at the ready. Several police cars had pulled up outside the main gate, and officers with sniffer dogs were crossing the forecourt.

"Oh, Simon!" she wailed. "Where are you?"

***

Simon had tried one door after another but had found only locked doors, storerooms and linen cupboards. He was beginning to think the others were right and he would never find the queen when he felt a ringing in his ears. Suddenly all the little sounds were back: the drone of distant traffic, a dog barking somewhere far away, muted conversations. Then a door opened at the far end of the corridor and a voice said, "Thank you, ma'am," and out came a butler carrying a tall silver teapot on a tray.

Simon waited until the butler had gone, then knocked on the door. Inside, dogs started yapping.

"Come in!" called a shrill voice.

Simon entered. It was an office. There were

filing cabinets around the walls, the floor was strewn with papers, and peering out from behind a computer screen was the queen. Her eyes were large behind her glasses.

"Hello!" said Simon.

The queen looked Simon up and down. "Hello," she said. "And who might you be?"

"I'm Simon Grubb," said Simon.

"How did you get here?"

"Through the door marked PRIVATE."

The queen removed her glasses and peered at Simon. "Did no one try to stop you?"

"No," said Simon. "*I* stopped *them*."

"I see," said the queen. But it was clear that she didn't.

"I stopped time," explained Simon. He took the stopwatch out of his pocket. "It's magic. I'll show you, if you like."

"I'd love to see your magic trick," said the queen. "But I'm afraid I don't have time."

"Yes, you do," said Simon. "You've got all the time you want, now."

"If only that were true."

"It is!"

The queen stood up and reached for Simon's hand. "Come along, young man," she said. "Let's go and find your mother."

Simon took the queen's hand. Then he said, "Time is motion," and pressed the button on the stopwatch.

Instantly, the corgis stopped panting. The clock on the mantelpiece stopped ticking. The sound of distant traffic disappeared. Only a thick, muffled silence remained. The queen frowned. She waggled a finger in her ear and opened and closed her mouth. "What happened?" she asked.

"I've stopped time," said Simon.

The queen glanced at her watch. Then she looked at her dogs. All three of them were standing as stiff as stuffed animals, with eyes like buttons. "My dogs!" she cried. "What's wrong with my dogs?"

"Don't worry," said Simon. "They'll come back to life when time starts up again."

"Starts up again?" said the queen faintly. She went to the window and threw it open. All of London was silent. The queen replaced her glasses and looked at Simon properly for the first time. "Magic, you say?"

Simon nodded.

The queen went to the door and looked left and right along the corridor. "Is anyone there?" she called. There was no reply. Cautiously, she ventured out. Simon followed. They hadn't gone far when they encountered the butler with the silver teapot on a tray. "Johnson?" said the queen.

Johnson did not move. The queen went close and tapped his shoulder. "*Johnson?*"

Nothing.

"Good grief!" said the queen. "Has everybody stopped?"

"Everyone but us," said Simon.

"How absolutely marvelous!"

It was as though the queen had woken from a long, long sleep and was seeing everything for the very first time. On the landing, she pirouetted in a slant of sunshine, then she paused to admire a pigeon suspended in mid-flight just outside the window. "What beautiful feathers it has," she

remarked. "Like rainbows on an oily puddle."
When they came to a group of tourists standing
motionless in the White Drawing Room, the
queen circled them slowly. "Remarkable!" she
said. Then the queen took Simon to the kitchen.
"I've never been down here," she said.

The kitchen was full of chefs who had frozen
in the middle of mixing, stirring and chopping.
Simon and the queen wandered around, dipping
their fingers into cake batter, soups and sauces.

Then the queen opened a fridge and drank some orange juice straight from the carton. "I feel ever so naughty," she said. "Don't you?"

"Not really," said Simon.

The queen sighed. "You're probably used to doing whatever you like. But I'm not."

"But you're the queen!" said Simon. "You can do whatever you want."

"Don't you believe it! There's always someone telling me what to do and where to go. They even tell me what to wear."

"It's the same for me," said Simon. "They never let me go out on my own."

"Me neither!" said the queen.

"They say I need looking after."

"And me!" cried the queen.

"— and whenever we go in the car," said Simon, "I never get to ride up front. I always have to sit in the back."

"So do I!" said the queen. She sighed. Then she said, "Tell me, Simon, do you like ice-cream sundaes?"

"Yes."

"Me, too," said the queen. So she rolled up her sleeves and went through the kitchen, opening cupboards and freezers. Together they filled an enormous crystal bowl with a mountain of ice cream in various flavors. Then they smothered the ice cream with whipped cream, strawberry sauce, maraschino cherries, chocolate sprinkles and miniature marshmallows. Finally, the queen stuck in two long-handled silver spoons. "Let's eat this in the garden," she said, and she picked up the bowl with both hands and carried it outside.

They had left the kitchen just in time. As the queen set down the bowl on a wrought-iron table, the birds began singing, the wind moved in the trees and a blackbird flew into the bushes with a trill of alarm.

Time had started up again.

CHAPTER 12

THE MAGIC CAMERA

"I don't get it," Jake said, glancing at his watch. "Where *is* he? Why doesn't he just stop time again?"

"For all we know," said Hannah, "he has."

They thought of Simon, wandering lost and lonely through the seven hundred and seventy-five rooms of Buckingham Palace. It could take him days to look in all of them. Sooner or later, he would have to give up. Time would start again. They'd be arrested and escorted from the palace through a crowd of reporters. Their parents would see them on the six o'clock news — and so would everyone at school. Hannah glanced at her monster-feet slippers. "Look at me!" she cried. "I'm not even dressed!"

Jake pointed his camera at Hannah and pressed the button.

"Don't!" said Hannah, making a grab for the camera.

"Chill!" said Jake, holding it out of reach. "I'm not taking pictures. I'm trying to figure out how this thing works."

"Why don't you figure out how to get us out of here instead?"

"I *am*. This thing is supposed to be magic. Philippe Fontaine gave it to me."

"Magic?" Hannah looked at the camera with interest. "You didn't tell me he'd given you a camera, too. What does it do?"

"Nothing. I think it's broken."

"Perhaps you're not doing it right."

"Of course I'm doing it right!" said Jake. "Try it yourself if you don't believe me."

He passed her the camera. It was large and heavy and had a lens like the end of a telescope, which you could turn to focus. Hannah put the strap around her neck. There was a fine black crosshair on the viewfinder, which made looking through the camera feel like looking down the barrel of a gun. Hannah moved the black cross around the room until it came to rest on Jake's frowning face. "What happens if I press the button?"

"Nothing."

Hannah pressed it. There was a loud click, but, somewhat to Hannah's relief, nothing happened. She pressed it a few more times, just to be sure. "Didn't the magician give you any instructions?"

"Nope. All he said was that it was a magic camera and that it would put me in the picture."

"What picture?"

Jake shrugged. " 'Straight from the brochure to the poolside,' " he said, " 'the Magic Camera puts you in the picture.' "

Hannah moved the black cross around the room until it settled on the painting above the mantel. It was an oil painting of an old English galleon in full sail. There was a little brass plaque set into the frame that said *Falcon —1578.* Hannah turned the lens slightly, and the painting came sharply into focus. She zoomed in until she could see the sea spray leaping over the decks. It was so realistic that she almost felt that she was really there, on the deck of the *Falcon.* "Straight from the brochure to the poolside," she murmured. "The Magic Camera puts you in the ..."

Hannah froze. Slowly, she lowered the camera. Her face was pale.

"What's up?" said Jake.

"I nearly took a picture of that picture!"

"So?"

"Don't you see?" said Hannah. "The Magic Camera puts you *in* the picture. If I'd pressed that button, I could have gone *into the painting.*"

Jake looked at the *Falcon* uncertainly. "But it's only a painting," he said. "It's not a photograph."

"Who said it had to be a photograph?"

Hannah imagined standing on deck in just her fluffy pink robe and monster-feet slippers. What would her parents have said when Jake told them that she was stuck in an oil painting and that if they ever wanted to see her again they'd have to buy the painting and hang it in their front room?

"I *knew* that magician was bad news," said Jake. He reached for the camera. "Give it here."

"What? Why?"

"I'm going to smash it. It's dangerous."

"Just a minute," said Hannah. "Let's think about this."

"What's to think about? Who wants to get stuck in a picture for the rest of their lives?"

"But we wouldn't get stuck," said Hannah. "Not if we took a picture *with* us to come back to." The more she thought about it, the more thrilling it was. It was almost as good as the magic carpet. They could go anywhere in the world — anywhere they had a picture of, at least — and come back again at the click of a button.

"What do you mean?" said Jake.

"If it works the way I think it does," said Hannah, "as long as we take a picture of *here* with us, we can come back whenever we want."

"We don't have a picture of here," said Jake.

"Yes, we do!" Hannah took the map out of her pocket. On the front was a photograph of the White Drawing Room.

"I guess we could try it," said Jake uncertainly.

"Why not? We can come back later, when the coast is clear."

Voices were approaching along the corridor. "Quickly!" said Hannah. "They're coming." She put the camera to her eye and aimed the black cross at the painting. "Ready?" she said.

Jake linked his arm in hers. "Ready!"

Hannah pressed the button, and everything went black.

CHAPTER 13

TIME IS MONEY

The more they talked, the more Simon and the queen found they had in common. They both loved watching television on Saturday mornings, and they both loved dogs, ice cream and magic tricks. The queen told Simon about her horses and her corgis, and Simon told the queen all about his mother and Jake and their house in Canada.

"What about your father?" said the queen. "Where is he?"

"In prison," said Simon.

"Dear me!" exclaimed the queen.

Simon explained that they were staying with

their aunt Helen and uncle Robert because their house had been repossessed by the bank.

"How awful!" said the queen.

"The worst thing," said Simon, "was leaving Monty behind."

"Who's Monty?"

"Our dog. Our neighbors have him now. They take him walking on a leash."

The Queen looked sad. "It's funny, isn't it? Your mother needs more money and I need more time. And people say that time is money — *pfft*!" She was thoughtful for a while, and in the pause they heard a voice calling from the far side of the garden: "*Your Majesty …! Your Majesty …!*"

"You see what I mean?" said the queen. "Never a moment to myself. I wonder what the problem is now?"

"There you are!" gasped Johnson, hurrying toward them. "I must ask that you come inside, ma'am."

"Whatever for?"

"Security has been breached, Your Majesty. Two children are running riot in your private quarters." Johnson glanced suspiciously at Simon, who busied himself with the ice-cream sundae.

"Surely children don't pose much of a threat, Johnson?" said the queen. "Can't we finish our ice cream while you deal with them?"

"I'm afraid not, ma'am."

The queen sighed. "Very well," she said. "Come along, Simon." She got to her feet and took Simon by the hand. Then suddenly she shouted, "Goodness! What's that?"

Johnson looked. While his back was turned, the queen picked up the stopwatch from the table. "Time is motion!" she said, and pressed the button.

Instantly, everything was still. The birds were silent, the breeze died and Johnson was frozen in position. The queen let go of Simon's hand and they sat back down again.

"Two children!" said the queen. "I wonder who they are?"

"It's probably Jake and Hannah," Simon said.

The queen looked at Simon in surprise. "Your brother? And your cousin? Dear me! Do you think we ought to go and find them?"

"No," said Simon, popping another cherry into his mouth. "We can do it later."

"I suppose you're right," said the queen. "After all, they won't be going anywhere, will they?"

"Nope," said Simon. "Not until the stopwatch gets to zero."

They both laughed.

CHAPTER 14

ALL ABOARD THE *FALCON*

In the darkness the floor seemed to tilt, and when Hannah released the button, she and Jake found themselves sprawled across the wooden deck of the *Falcon*. They scrambled to their feet. A bright, strong wind was blowing, and the air was loud with flapping sails and crashing waves. As far as they could see in every direction there was nothing but the heaving ocean. Buckingham Palace suddenly seemed impossibly remote. It was clear that they had made a terrible mistake, and as though to prove it, a wave crashed up over the bulwark, drenching them both.

"Let's go back!" shouted Hannah.

Jake nodded.

Hannah got the map out of her pocket. It snapped and cracked in the wind like a live thing.

"Give it here," said Jake.

But just as Hannah was passing it, the wind snatched the map right out of her hands.

"No!" yelled Jake. "No!"

They stumbled after it, but the map blew over the forecastle and out to sea. There was nothing they could do but watch as the wind carried it up, up and away like a kite without a string. Soon it was just a speck in the sky.

They were still looking at it when a shout went up: "Stowaways!"

The children looked around. To their alarm, they saw the crew of the *Falcon* rushing toward them from all directions. In no time, they were surrounded by grubby sailors wearing felt hats, britches and billowing white shirts. Two of them were pointing muskets.

"Put your hands up!" said one of the men.

"Watch out!" said another. "This one has a gun."

"It's not a gun," said Hannah. "It's a camera."

But the men paid no attention. They snatched the camera and rummaged in the pockets of Hannah's robe.

"Ahoy!" said a sailor, finding the potato. "What's this?"

"It's a potato," said Hannah miserably.

"A what?"

Before Hannah could explain, another man appeared. He had a pointy little beard and a feather in his cap. "What's going on here?" he demanded.

"Pirates, Sir Walter," said one of the sailors.

Sir Walter Raleigh put his hands on his hips and looked the children up and down. His eyes widened when he saw Hannah's monster-feet slippers.

"Please, sir, we aren't pirates," said Hannah. "We lost our map. If you could —"

"Take them below!" barked Sir Walter.

***

In a tiny cabin behind the galley, Horatio lay
groaning in his bunk. He had already been sick
so many times that he had nothing left inside
him, but he still felt like throwing up. How long
would he have to spend in this creaky old tub
before they reached the promised lands of the
New World? Weeks? Months? He would probably
die before they got there. In fact, he felt so ill he
didn't care if he *did* die.

Horatio was sorry he'd ever volunteered to
be a cabin boy on the *Falcon*. All he'd wanted
was to be an explorer, like his hero, Sir Walter
Raleigh. But life at sea was not at all like he'd
imagined. The biscuits were full of maggots, and
the sailors were nasty, dirty men with terrible
manners. Worst of all, the ceaseless tilt and roll
of the ship made Horatio seasick. The only
tolerable job on board the *Falcon* was keeping
a lookout from the crow's nest. Up there, with
the wind in his hair and his arms outstretched,

Horatio had felt as if he were flying. But after he had vomited onto a group of sailors scrubbing the decks, he hadn't been allowed to keep watch again. Now they only let him scrub the decks and empty chamber pots.

Just then, Horatio's thoughts were interrupted by raised voices in the corridor. He sat up. What was going on? Were they under attack by pirates? Had they spied land? Horatio rolled out of his bunk and struggled into his hat and jacket. He opened the door just as several sailors went past. "What's happening?" he said.

"Stowaways!" said one of the sailors.

"Pirates, I reckon!" said another.

"Oh," said Horatio, disappointed. "I thought we were nearly there."

The sailors laughed. "Feeling a little peaky, are we?" said one. He put his finger down his throat and made gagging noises.

Horatio gave the sailor a withering look. He waited until they had passed then ventured along the corridor to the Great Cabin. The door was ajar, and Horatio could hear the voices of

Sir Walter Raleigh, Sir Humphrey Gilbert and Reverend Bull within.

"Do you really think they're pirates?" came Sir Humphrey's voice.

"They don't look much like pirates to me," replied Sir Walter. "Did you see what the girl has on her feet?"

"I did," said Sir Humphrey. "I've never seen the like in all my travels."

"Nor I," said Sir Walter. "Do you think it's possible that they're from the New World?"

"Well, if they are," said Reverend Bull, "I don't see how they came aboard. There isn't a ship in sight."

"They *claim*," said Sir Walter, "that this contraption is their means of transport. But I can't see how it works."

Horatio put his head around the door and saw the men examining something with a single glass eye and a long strap.

"It looks like some sort of optical instrument," said Sir Humphrey. "But it seems to make everything smaller."

"It's a portable firearm," said Reverend Bull. "Look. It says *Canon*, right here."

"And what about *that* curiosity?" said Sir Humphrey, pointing at the potato.

"It's a serpent's egg," said Reverend Bull.

"That's no egg," said Sir Walter. "It's a tuber."

"Here," said Reverend Bull, "I'll cut it open with my — *oops!*"

The potato fell to the floor. It bounced
twice and went rolling first to one side of
the cabin, then the other, as the ship pitched.
Then it disappeared under a cabinet and stayed
there. The men got down on their knees.

"You fool!" said Sir Walter. "It's gone right
to the back."

"I can't quite …"

"Stop! You'll push it farther in!"

While they were trying to retrieve the potato,
Horatio tiptoed into the room, picked up the
camera and peered into the lens. His own pale
face was reflected back at him. Now was his
chance. His ticket to the New World was right
here, in his hands! But he would have to act
quickly. With a thumping heart, he clutched the
camera to his chest, slipped out of the room
and hurried back along the corridor.

CHAPTER 15

ABANDON SHIP

Hannah and Jake were locked in a cabin containing nothing but a writing desk and a chair. There was a tiny latticed window through which they glimpsed the ocean one minute and the sky the next, as the ship pitched. The battering of the waves upon the hull sounded like thunder.

"I think I'm going to be sick," groaned Hannah.

"Look at the horizon, then," said Jake.

Hannah went to the window. How strange it was to think that somewhere out there, in the future, the police would be searching for them in Buckingham Palace. Only moments ago, being found by the police had felt like the worst thing that could happen. But how happy she would be to be found by the police now! Tears sprang to Hannah's eyes as she thought of her parents appearing on the news, making an appeal for information. Yet no matter how hard they searched, nobody would ever find them here.

"My mother was right," said Hannah tearfully. "She said you were trouble."

Jake, who was sitting at the desk with his head in his hands, looked up. "That's rich," he said. "*You're* the one who got us into trouble."

"Me?"

"You're the one who wanted to go into the picture. I don't know why I listened to you. In fact, I should never have let you come with us in the first place."

Hannah flushed. She had forgotten that the ship had been her idea. "You're right," she said. "I'm sorry. It was a stupid thing to do."

Jake sighed. "It's my fault, too," he admitted. "If I hadn't been going to rob the Bank of England, none of this would have happened."

Hannah stared at him. "You were going to rob the Bank of England?"

"Just a couple of gold bars."

"But that's stealing!" said Hannah, shocked. She suddenly remembered the jewelry store. "You were going to take one of those necklaces, too, weren't you?"

Jake said nothing.

"And that's why you were asking my father about the Crown Jewels, wasn't it?"

Jake was silent.

"That's all you care about!" cried Hannah. "Money! What do you need it for, anyway?"

"It's not for me," said Jake.

"Who, then?"

"My mom."

All at once, Hannah understood. Jake wanted to give Aunt Rachel the money so that she could buy their house. Then they wouldn't have to move or give Monty away or change schools. And they'd still be able to visit their father.

"I was only trying to help," said Jake. "But now I'll never see them again." He folded his arms on the table and buried his face. His shoulders began to shake. Hannah began sobbing, too. Soon they were blubbering so loudly that neither of them heard someone slip quietly into the room and lock the door.

"Ahem!" said a voice.

Startled, they turned and saw a gangly youth wearing grubby white leggings and a jacket with puffed sleeves. He removed his hat and bowed low. "Horatio Montague," he said. "Pleased to make your acquaintance."

Jake quickly wiped his eyes with his sleeve. "I'm Jake," he said.

"And I'm Hannah," said Hannah.

Horatio glanced at Hannah's robe and monster-feet slippers. "Is it true?" he said. "Are you really from the New World?"

"You could say that," said Jake.

Horatio's face lit up. "I knew it! How far away are we?"

"About five hundred years," said Jake, glumly.

Horatio's face fell. "Impossible! If it's so far away, how did *you* get here?"

"We had a magic camera," said Jake, "but they confiscated it."

Horatio opened his jacket. "Is this it?"

"Yes!" Jake reached for the camera, but Horatio quickly closed his jacket.

"Not so fast!" Horatio said. "I'll return it … on one condition."

"What's that?" said Jake.

"You must take me back with you."

"The trouble is," said Hannah, tearfully, "the camera won't work on its own. We also need a picture of the place we want to go to. We had one, but it blew away."

"Can't you draw another?" said Horatio, pointing to the quill pen on the desk.

For a moment, Hannah and Jake both stared at the pen. Then Jake snatched it up, seized a piece of parchment and began sketching.

"Do you think the camera will recognize it?" said Hannah eagerly.

"I don't know." Jake wiped away a large wet blot, smudging it across the paper. "How does the entrance go?"

"I think it's bigger than that. No, wider. And aren't there some columns?"

"Please hurry," said Horatio. "We haven't got much time."

Jake scratched a few more lines, then threw down the quill. "It's no good," he said. "It looks more like the White House than Buckingham Palace. I can't do it."

"Draw somewhere else, then," said Hannah. "Somewhere you *do* know. Anywhere!"

Jake turned the parchment over and began again. The others looked on as, slowly, the building acquired windows, a front door and a chimney. There were pine trees surrounding it and a large FOR SALE sign stuck in the lawn.

"It's *your* house!" said Hannah.

Jake was just drawing the front steps when the cabin door rattled. A voice said, "They've locked themselves in!"

"Quick! Give me the camera," hissed Jake.

"NO!" said Horatio. "*I'll* do it."

The rattling turned to banging, followed by heavy blows.

"All right, all right!" said Jake impatiently. "Aim the cross *here*. Then press the button."

Horatio put his eye to the viewfinder, and Jake and Hannah linked their arms in his. All three of them shuffled first to the left, and then to the right, as the ship rolled.

"Hurry!" cried Hannah.

The door burst open and Sir Walter Raleigh strode into the room, followed closely by Sir Humphrey and Reverend Bull. "Horatio!" said Sir Walter in surprise. "What are you —?"

Horatio pressed the button, and everything went black.

CHAPTER 16

AUNT RACHEL'S HOUSE

Hannah, Jake and Horatio found themselves standing arm in arm on the lawn in front of Aunt Rachel's house. A crow at the top of a pine tree flew off, cawing, surprised at their sudden appearance.

"It worked!" cried Hannah joyfully.

Jake extracted his arm from Horatio's, ran up the path, got the key out from under the mat and let himself in. The others followed him.

Now that it was empty, the house felt strange. The pictures had been removed from the walls. There were no coats hanging on the pegs in the hall. The kitchen cupboards were empty, and cardboard boxes were stacked on the counters with PLATES or SPICES written on them in black marker pen. Even the plants seemed to have stopped growing in Aunt Rachel's absence.

Jake went to the window and stood looking out across the garden to the path that led down to the river.

"Now what?" said Hannah, coming up behind him.

Jake shrugged. "Go back to London, I guess."

"How?"

Without answering, Jake turned and headed for the stairs. Hannah followed, and Horatio, who'd been flicking the light switch on and off, flicked it one last time and then hurried after them.

Jake's bedroom was unrecognizable. The bed had been removed, leaving dusty floorboards. The shelves were empty, the walls were bare and there were boxes stacked in the middle of the room with GAMES, SCHOOL STUFF and BEDDING written on them. Jake opened a box marked BOOKS. "I think I've got a photo album in one of these boxes," he said. "There might be a picture of your house in it."

He tipped up the box, and the books slid onto the floor. There were *Archie* comics and *National Geographic* magazines and lots of illustrated books with titles like *Wolves* and *The Vikings* and *The Story of Flight*. But there were no photo albums.

"It must be in another one," said Hannah.

While they were opening the next box, Horatio flipped through the books. He kept pointing at pictures of cars, trains, airplanes and bicycles and asking, "What's this?" and "What's that?" Eventually, he picked up a book called *Exploring Space*. On the front was a picture of an astronaut sitting in a rocket. "What's this man doing?" he asked.

Jake glanced at the book impatiently. "He's an astronaut. He's exploring outer space."

"Outer *space?*" said Horatio.

Jake waved toward the window. "Up there. Above the clouds."

While the others continued searching for the photo album, Horatio studied pictures of the rings of Jupiter, meteors with fiery tails and planet Earth suspended in the darkness like a blue-green Christmas bauble.

"Here it is!" said Jake at last, pulling his album out from beneath the World Atlas. He and Hannah turned the pages hopefully. But it was immediately clear that none of the photographs would do. Either Hannah or Jake or Simon was in every one.

"We can't go into a picture where we already *are*," said Hannah. "Something terrible might happen."

"And even if we *weren't* in the picture," Jake pointed out, "we'd still be going back in time."

This was something they hadn't considered. Neither of them wanted to end up in the past again.

Jake closed the album. "We'll have to go next door," he said, "and ask the Reillys if we can call your parents."

Hannah nodded. Her parents would find it difficult to understand how they had traveled all the way to Canada, but they had no choice. Jake chucked the album back onto the pile. But just then, another book caught Hannah's eye. It was the World Atlas. "Wait a minute," she said. "What about this? Will the camera take us someplace on a map, do you think?"

"I don't know," said Jake.

Hannah looked up "Buckingham Palace" in the index. There were two page numbers, and the second reference was for a road map of the center of London. The map showed the River Thames, with all the bridges, and there were even tiny drawings of the major landmarks. Hannah recognized St. Paul's Cathedral and the Houses of Parliament. Buckingham Palace was there, too, by Hyde Park Corner.

"Let's try it," said Hannah. "Come on, Horatio."

Horatio looked up, startled. "What?"

"We're going back to London," said Hannah.

Horatio stood up, clutching *Exploring Space*. "No," he said. "I won't go. I want to stay in the New World."

"It's *all* the new world, now," said Jake. "You're in the future."

Horatio's eyes widened. "I'm in the future?"

"Yes! Now let's get out of here." Jake found a pen and drew an *X* on the map, just in front of Buckingham Palace. Then he propped the atlas open on the windowsill. "Aim the black cross here," he said. "And be careful. We don't want to end up in the Thames."

Horatio put *Exploring Space* back on the floor. Then he lifted the camera to his eye, went close to the map and adjusted the focus. Hannah and Jake both linked their arms in his.

"Ready?" said Horatio.

Jake looked around his bedroom one last time and took a deep breath. He nodded. "Ready," he said.

CHAPTER 17

LONDON

The next moment, the children landed — *whump*!
— face down in a flower bed near the Victoria
Monument. Groaning, they got to their feet.
Hannah had had the wind knocked out of her,
and Horatio's hat had fallen off.

"What happened?" gasped Hannah, securing
the belt of her robe.

"I guess the camera had to set us down flat,"
said Jake. He shook the dirt out of his hair. "A
map is only two dimensional, after all."

"Where are we?" said Horatio, replacing his
hat. "And why is everything so quiet?"

The others looked around. London was completely silent. Nothing moved.

"Time has stopped," said Hannah.

"That means Simon's still here," said Jake. "Quick! We've got to find him before time starts again." He set off toward the main gate at a run. Hannah grabbed Horatio's sleeve, and they hurried after him.

A crowd was standing motionless outside the gate, along with several news reporters, a camera crew and a police officer wearing a high-visibility jacket. Cautiously, the children edged through them. Horatio's puffed sleeves were rather bulky though, and when he brushed against a large man wearing shorts with knee-high socks, the man began to wobble. Fortunately, Hannah and Jake managed to set him on his feet again before he sent the whole crowd toppling like dominoes.

Eventually, they made it to the gate. They ran across the forecourt, in through the Grand Entrance and up the red-carpeted stairs two at a time. Hannah caught a glimpse of herself in one of the enormous mirrors. Instead of the timid-looking girl she had seen reflected earlier, she now saw a wild thing with windswept hair and a filthy robe. But there wasn't time to worry about that. They flew through the Portrait Gallery and the Ballroom and the West Gallery, shouting: "SIMON! SIMON!" But there was no sign of him.

Eventually they stopped, breathless.

"He's got to be here somewhere," said Hannah. "Unless he's gone home. You don't think he —"

"Shhh!" said Jake. "Listen."

Faintly, in the distance, they heard voices. Jake opened a set of French doors and stepped outside. From across the garden came the sound of laughter.

"It's him!" said Jake.

They hurried across the lawn and through a gap in the hedge — and there was Simon. He was sitting at a wrought-iron table with an elderly lady. Between them were the remains of afternoon tea: a silver stand crowded with tiny sandwiches with the crusts cut off, a plate of cake crumbs and a pot of tea. Two corgis barked as they approached.

"Simon!" said Jake. "What are you —?"

The lady turned around.

"Er … Hi," said Jake.

"Your Majesty!" said Hannah, shocked.

"Jake! And Hannah!" said the queen. "It's a pleasure to meet you. I've heard so much about you." The queen looked at Horatio then, in his wrinkled leggings and puffed sleeves. "And who is this?"

"Horatio Montague, Your Majesty." Horatio removed his hat with a flourish and bowed low. "Sir Walter Raleigh's cabin boy."

"We got him from your painting," explained Hannah.

"I see," said the queen, who looked as though nothing could surprise her now. "Would you care to join us for a cucumber sandwich?"

"Thank you," said Hannah. "But we must get home. First, though, we need to take Horatio back to the *Falcon*."

Horatio clutched the camera to his chest. "I'm not going back there," he said, aghast.

"But you have to!" said Hannah. "Where else will you go?"

"I'll come with you."

"Oh, no, you won't," said Jake.

Horatio looked hurt. "But you promised."

"We did *not* promise," said Jake. "We said you could come *back* with us. We didn't say that you could *stay* with us."

"Oh, dear," murmured the queen.

"Even if we wanted you to stay," said Hannah, "our parents wouldn't let you."

"She's right," said Jake.

"And anyway," said Hannah. "What about *your* parents? Won't they wonder where you are?"

"I don't have parents," said Horatio sadly. "I have benefactors. They won't miss me."

"What about your friends, then?" said Hannah.

"I don't have any friends," said Horatio. His chin began to tremble, and he took out a filthy handkerchief and blew his nose.

Hannah looked at Horatio helplessly. "All right," she said. "You can come with us. But only until we figure out what to do with you, okay?"

Horatio cheered up instantly. "Aye aye, Captain," he said.

"Come on, Simon," said Jake. "Let's go."

"Do we have to?" said Simon. He had ice cream all around his mouth.

"Yes," said Jake. "We do."

Simon belched softly, got down off his chair and threw his arms around the queen. "Thank you for having me," he said.

The queen hugged him back. "No, Simon," she said. "Thank *you*."

"Goodbye, Your Majesty!" said Hannah.

"Goodbye," said the queen. She waved until the children were out of sight. Then she took the stopwatch out of her pocket and checked the digital display. "I wonder how long we can stop time for?" she mused. "I think we're due for a little holiday. What do you say, girls?"

The corgis barked in agreement.

CHAPTER 18

THE NEW WORLD

Hannah, Jake, Simon and Horatio went out
through the palace gate and picked their way
back through the crowd. But as they were
collecting their bikes, they felt their ears pop,
and suddenly the world was moving at full tilt
again. Horatio clung to Hannah, startled by the
roar of passing cars.

"Where's the stopwatch, Simon?" said Jake.

"I don't have it," said Simon.

"What do you mean, you don't have it?
Where is it?"

"I gave it to the queen."

Hannah groaned.

"The queen?" cried Jake. "What did you give it to *her* for? She's already got everything she could possibly want!"

"She doesn't have time."

"She's got exactly the same amount of time as the rest of us," said Jake.

"Not to herself she doesn't."

Jake was furious. "You'll have to go back," he said, "and tell her it was a mistake."

"He can't do that," objected Hannah. "You can't take something back once you've given it away. And anyway, we'd never get into the palace now."

Of course, Hannah was right. Jake did try, but his way was barred by the police officer at the gate. "Sorry, son," said the officer. "The palace is closed this afternoon. There's been an incident."

"I don't want to see the palace," said Jake impatiently. "I want to see the queen. She knows me. Ask her, if you don't believe me."

The officer smirked. "If you know her so well," he said, "why don't you give her a call?"

The crowd chuckled.

"Send her a text!" said the man wearing shorts and knee-socks.

The laughter grew until Jake retreated, red-faced.

"I told you they wouldn't listen," said Hannah. "We might as well go home."

So they set off on their bikes, with Horatio perched on Jake's handlebars. But when they got to the main road, the traffic made it too dangerous to cycle, so they all dismounted and wheeled their bikes along the sidewalk.

"My parents have probably called the police by now," said Hannah gloomily.

They walked as quickly as they could, but Horatio kept stopping to look at things. He was intrigued by the cartoons playing on a TV in a store window. He eavesdropped on a man talking on a phone and pointed at a woman with pink hair. Simon wheeled his bicycle at Horatio's side, explaining everything like a miniature tour guide, while Hannah and Jake walked on ahead.

"What are we going to *do* with him?" hissed Hannah.

"*I* don't know. You're the one who said he could come with us."

"What was I supposed to say? We couldn't just abandon him."

"Well, he came *out* of a picture," said Jake. "Why don't we send him back into a picture?"

"What sort of picture?"

"That sort?" They were passing a drugstore, and in the window there was an advertisement for tissues, featuring a basket of fluffy white kittens.

"Don't be ridiculous," said Hannah.

"Or we could send him there." Jake pointed to a poster on the side of a bus shelter. It was an advertisement for underarm deodorant and it showed a roller coaster full of people with their arms in the air.

"That's just mean," said Hannah.

They walked on, deep in thought. "There must be *somewhere* he can go," said Hannah. "It would have to be a safe place, though. Somewhere he can make friends and have adventures and nobody will wonder where his parents are. Somewhere he can be free."

"The only places like that," said Jake dryly, "are in books."

Hannah gasped. "That's it! A book!"

"What?" said Jake.

"We'll send him into a book."

"What sort of book?"

"A children's book."

"A fairy tale, you mean?"

"No!" Hannah shuddered. "Horrid things happen in fairy tales. I was thinking of somewhere more like Narnia. Or what about *Winnie-the-Pooh*? Or *Charlie and the Chocolate Factory*?"

Jake looked doubtful. "What if he doesn't want to go?"

"Why wouldn't he? You can do what you like in a book. Nothing *really* awful ever happens, and there's always a happy ending."

"It's not a bad idea," admitted Jake. He almost looked as though he wished he could go into a book himself.

"Anyway," said Hannah, "it's Horatio who has to decide. Let's ask him."

They turned around. Simon and Horatio were outside the Cinema Deluxe. They appeared to be discussing a poster showing a spaceship flying past an enormous orange planet. The poster was advertising a film called *The New World*.

"SIMON!" yelled Jake.

Horatio looked directly at them. Then he ducked into the Cinema Deluxe. Jake cursed. He and Hannah turned their bikes around and made their way back to Simon.

"*Now* where's he gone?" said Jake.

"He said he wanted to see *The New World*," said Simon.

"We'd better go and get him," said Hannah. So they propped their bikes against the wall and went into the theater. The lobby was full of people milling about. But where was Horatio?

"There he is!" said Simon, pointing.

"HORATIO!" Jake yelled.

Horatio turned and ran straight past the ticket collector and into Theater Three.

"After him!" said Jake.

But the ticket collector barred the way. "Oh, no, you don't!" he said. "Tickets, please!"

"We don't want to see the film," explained Hannah. "We only want to find our friend."

"No ticket, no entry. That's the rule."

"All right, all right," said Jake. "One ticket, please."

"I'm coming, too," said Simon.

"And you're not leaving *me* behind," said Hannah.

"Three tickets, then," said Jake.

"Four," said the ticket collector. "Don't forget your friend."

Since Jake was the only one with money, he had to take off his shoe and spend his emergency £20 bill. Then they all went through the doors into Theater Three.

CHAPTER 19

ALL IS LOST

It was dark inside the theater. There were a few teenagers eating popcorn at the back, some children with their parents … and Horatio. He was sitting on his own near the front, with his mouth agape and the light from the screen flickering across his astonished face.

"Wait here," Jake said. "I'll go and get him."

The others watched as Jake edged down the row. When he reached Horatio there was a short exchange. Jake took hold of Horatio's arm, but Horatio shrugged him off.

"Sit down!" said someone in the row behind.

Horatio jumped up and ran along the row. Toward the end, a man and his daughter were eating popcorn. Horatio leaped over them, sending popcorn flying into the air.

"Hey!" yelled the man.

"Security!" called someone else.

The doors opened, and a security guard rushed in. Horatio turned and sprinted up the aisle, but the guard ran after him and caught him by the collar. Horatio twisted free and ran along an empty row, but a second guard was advancing from the other end. Horatio was trapped. There was no escape.

Or was there?

Slowly, Horatio turned toward the screen and put the camera to his eye.

"NO!" cried Jake.

"No photos!" yelled the guard. He rushed at Horatio and made a grab for the camera. But to his surprise, his hand closed on nothing but thin air. The guard looked around, confused. The boy had vanished! He shone his flashlight under all the seats and into the row behind. There was no one there. Only the grubby felt hat in the aisle was evidence that Horatio had been there at all.

But Hannah, Jake and Simon knew where he had gone. They were watching the film. Horatio was at the controls of the spaceship, and he seemed to be looking directly at them from the screen. He grinned and waved. Simon waved back. Then the spaceship turned and sped off at the speed of light. And that was the last they saw of Horatio Montague and the Magic Camera.

Hannah, Jake and Simon weren't able to slip away so easily. They were escorted to the manager's office. "Are you sending us to jail?" asked Simon.

"No," said the manager. "I'm calling your parents."

Hannah gave him her phone number, and they had to sit and listen while the manager called her father and told him everything. Then they had to wait until he came to pick them up.

"It wasn't our fault," said Hannah, as her father put their bikes on the roof rack. "We were only —"

"Save it, Hannah," said her father. "You can explain everything when we get home. And it had better be good. Your mother has been out of her mind with worry."

Hannah climbed into the car. They were just like those children in stories, she thought — the ones who get three wishes and then waste them all on stupid things. First they had let the carpet get wet. Then they had given away the stopwatch. Now the camera was gone — and they had only themselves to blame. Hannah hoped that the magic carpet would be all right when it dried out. She sat back miserably and glanced at Jake. He had his arm round Simon, but his face was turned toward the window, so it was impossible to know what he was thinking. Only Simon seemed untroubled; he was sound asleep.

CHAPTER 20

THE QUEEN

Unfortunately, Hannah had forgotten that it was Friday, the day for garbage collection. The trucks had come by while they were out, and the first thing Hannah noticed as they pulled up outside their house was that the carpet was gone.

"Oh, no!" wailed Hannah, jumping out of the car. "They've taken the carpet!"

"What carpet?" said her father.

"A magician gave it to us," said Jake. "We left it right there, by the wall."

"Well, that was silly," said Hannah's father. "I expect it's at the dump by now."

"Let's go!" cried Hannah. "We'll find it if we hurry."

"We're going nowhere," said Hannah's father crisply. "Get in the house before I lose my patience."

Hannah burst into tears.

"Hannah?" said her mother, coming out to meet them. She noticed Hannah's wild hair and filthy robe. "What's happened? Are you all right?"

"She's upset about a carpet," said Hannah's father. "The garbage collectors have taken it."

"Is that where they've been? Looking for a carpet?"

Aunt Rachel came to the door then, and Simon ran to her. She took his face between her hands. "Where have you been?" she said. "And what have you been eating?"

"We've been to see the queen," said Simon. He started telling her all about it, but it came out rushed and breathless and impossible to follow, the way it did when he was trying to tell her about a movie he had seen.

"What were you thinking, Hannah?" said her mother reproachfully. "Going off on your bikes like that without telling anyone? You didn't even leave a note."

"It wasn't Hannah's fault," said Jake. "It was my idea."

Aunt Rachel sighed. "I don't know what's got into you, Jake," she said. "I know you didn't want to come to London. It's been difficult for all of us. But if you give it a chance, you might even get to like it here."

"I already do," Jake muttered.

"Pardon me?" said Aunt Rachel.

"I said I already do like it here," said Jake.

"You do?"

Jake nodded. "I've been thinking about it. London isn't so bad. I'd rather be here than … some other places."

"Oh, Jake," said Aunt Rachel. "I hope that's true. As long as we stick together, that's all that matters."

And of course it *was* all that mattered. When Hannah thought about how close they'd come to never seeing their parents again, she felt sick. She glanced at Jake, but he avoided looking at her, and she knew that he was thinking the same thing.

"Well, *I* want a full explanation," said Hannah's mother. "Everybody in the front room, please. Now!"

But just then they heard a cheerful honking. An enormous motor home was coming down the street. There were solar panels on the roof and a Union Jack flying from the aerial. Two corgis had their heads out the window.

"What on earth?" said Hannah's mother.

The motor home stopped outside their house. Out climbed a tanned old lady with wispy white curls. She was wearing a pale pink jogging suit and runners, with a matching visor.

"It's the queen!" said Simon.

The queen came up the garden path, carrying a handbag. "Good afternoon," she said, offering her hand. "You must be Mr. Jones."

"I am!" said Hannah's father, startled.

"And you must be Mrs. Jones?"

"Your Majesty," said Hannah's mother. She took the queen's hand and, uncertain as to what to do with it, she curtsied.

"And *you*," said the queen, turning to Aunt Rachel, "must be Mrs. Grubb. Simon has told me all about you."

"He has?" Aunt Rachel looked confused.

"Yes. In fact, he's the reason that I'm here."

"Dear me," groaned Hannah's father. "What's he done *now*?"

"Whatever it was," said Hannah's mother, "I'm sure he didn't mean it."

"Oh, I assure you, he did," said the queen.

"Please come in," Aunt Rachel said. "Let's talk about it."

"I'd like nothing better," said the queen. "But I can't let too much time pass, or they'll notice that I've gone. I just came to give you the deeds."

"Deeds?" said Aunt Rachel. "What deeds?"

"The deeds for your house." The queen rummaged in her handbag and brought out a large brown envelope. "Here they are. All you have to do is sign at the bottom, and the house is yours."

"I'm sorry," Aunt Rachel said, perplexed. "But I think there's been a mistake. Which house are you talking about?"

"*Your* house!" said the queen. "Simon told me that you didn't really want to move. So I thought, why not buy the house myself? I hope you don't mind."

"You bought our old house?" said Jake.

"Yes. And now I'm giving it to you."

There was a stunned silence.

"I don't understand," said Aunt Rachel. "It's very generous of you, but —"

"It's nothing," said the queen. "Not compared to what Simon's given me."

"What *did* Simon give you?"

"Time," said the queen.

"Well!" said Aunt Rachel, baffled. "Thank you. Thank you very much."

"It's my pleasure," said the queen. "And now I must get going."

"But wait —" said Hannah's mother. "I don't understand. Where did you meet the children?"

"Aha!" The queen tapped the side of her nose confidentially. "I'm afraid that information is Top Secret. Security reasons. I hope you understand."

"Of course. I didn't mean to pry."

"Of course not. Goodbye!"

A small crowd had gathered around the queen's motor home. The queen paused to sign several autographs and have her photo taken. Then Hannah's father opened the door, and the queen climbed into the driver's seat and put the window down. "Next time you're in the neighborhood," she said to Hannah and her parents, "you must come to the palace for afternoon tea. We do a lovely cucumber sandwich. Goodbye, Simon. I'll be in touch!" She gave the crowd a royal wave then drove off down the road, followed by several small children and a couple of dogs.

CHAPTER 21

BON VOYAGE

"I need to sit down," said Aunt Rachel. So they all went inside, and Aunt Rachel opened the envelope and removed the deeds. "It's true," she said. Her hands were trembling. "She's put the house in my name."

"Let me see," said Hannah's mother. But even she couldn't find anything wrong.

"We're going home," said Aunt Rachel, and to everyone's surprise, she burst into tears.

"What's the matter now?" said Jake.

"Nothing! Nothing at all!" Aunt Rachel said, laughing.

"Well!" Hannah's mother glanced at her watch. "I don't suppose we'll get to the museum now. We might as well have our sandwiches. It's nearly lunchtime."

Hannah's father unpacked the egg-and-cress sandwiches and they sat around with plates on their laps — all except for Simon, who was full. While they ate they talked about how soon they might be able to book a flight to Canada, whether it was too late to cancel the shipment of their boxes, and when they could arrange to collect Monty.

Hannah got up and went to the kitchen to put her plate in the sink. She was happy for Aunt Rachel and the boys, of course. But she couldn't help thinking about the magic carpet lying among all those broken electrical appliances and bags of garbage. Tears filled her eyes. It would have been better if she'd never seen it. At least then she wouldn't have known what she was missing.

***

Aunt Rachel booked a flight for the following Friday, which gave them a week to see the sights of London. But Hannah's enthusiasm for showing her cousins around had evaporated. She trailed after the rest of the family, thinking about the carpet and gazing vacantly at the exhibits in the Natural History Museum.

"What's the matter with you, Hannah?" her mother said. "Cheer up, won't you? I thought you were looking forward to having the boys here."

Hannah's father did his best, getting everyone to gather around while he read aloud from the *Pocket Guide to London*. But the boys weren't easily impressed. They'd seen the major landmarks already, and things generally look more exciting from a magic carpet than they do from the ground.

On Tuesday they took a tour of Buckingham Palace. Hannah and Jake wore sunglasses the whole time, afraid that one of the guards might recognize them. But Simon told his mother all about the kitchens and the gardens and the door behind the red curtain in the Throne Room.

"How come you're such an expert?" said Aunt Rachel, laughing. "Anyone would think you'd been here before!"

"I have," said Simon.

"He means he's taken a *virtual* tour," said Jake, shooting Simon a warning look.

On Wednesday they went on the London Eye, and on Thursday they climbed the 528 steps to the dome of St. Paul's Cathedral. "What do you think, boys?" said Hannah's father, from the Golden Gallery. "Ever been this high before?"

"Yes," said Simon.

The boys did enjoy the National Maritime Museum, though, somewhat to Aunt Rachel's surprise. She hadn't realized Jake knew so much about English galleons. Jake was keen to see the bronze statue of Sir Walter Raleigh in Greenwich, too; but when they got there, he said it looked nothing like him and that the real Sir Walter Raleigh had skinny legs.

"Jake's a bit of a know-it-all, isn't he?" said Hannah's father, when the boys were out of earshot.

"It's typical of the young these days," said Hannah's mother. "They've already seen it all online."

But when the following Friday came around, the boys could barely contain their excitement. Simon kept saying how happy Monty would be to see them, and all Jake could talk about was the canoeing trip that he could now go on with his friends.

After breakfast Aunt Rachel and the boys went upstairs to pack. Hannah was brushing her teeth when Jake came in to get his toothbrush. "I'm sorry about the carpet," he said.

Hannah spat into the sink. "It wasn't your fault."

"I know. I'm sorry you didn't get to ride it though."

"That's okay."

"When you visit us," said Jake, "we'll take you river rafting on an inner tube. It's just as good as the carpet. Better, even."

"Thanks," said Hannah. It was nice of him to say so, but she knew it wasn't true.

"And this time," said Jake, looking sheepish, "I promise not to leave you behind."

Hannah smiled. "Okay." But just as Jake was going out the door, she said, "Aren't you sorry that you lost your camera, though? And the stopwatch?"

Jake shrugged. "Not really. Going home is magic enough for me."

***

When their car had been loaded up, Aunt Rachel and the boys got in and put their windows down. "Come visit us soon, won't you?" said Aunt Rachel.

"We will," said Hannah's father.

"Bye!" said the boys.

Hannah and her parents stood and waved until Aunt Rachel's car had turned the corner and was gone.

"Well," said Hannah's mother, "I must admit I'm glad we're on our own again. Cup of tea?"

But just as Hannah and her father were about to follow her inside, Mrs. Miles from next door popped her head over the fence.

"Robert!" she said.

"Hello, Jean," said Hannah's father.

"Your sister-in-law has gone home, then?"

"Yes! A sudden change of fortune." Hannah's father started telling Mrs. Miles about the events of the previous week.

But Hannah wasn't listening. She was staring at something that was rolled up and leaning against Mrs. Miles's garden wall. "That's our carpet!" she cried.

"Oh, that old thing?" said Mrs. Miles. "I didn't think you'd mind me taking it, seeing as you were throwing it out. I've been looking for something to wipe my boots on when I come in from the garden. Unfortunately, it wasn't suitable."

"It wasn't?" said Hannah.

"No. It kept ruckling up. Twice it nearly tripped me. It's got a life of its own, that carpet. So I've put it out again."

Hannah turned to her father. "Can I keep it?"

Her father looked doubtful. "It's a bit shabby.

I don't know if your mother will want it in the house."

"*Please!* I'll clean it up."

"On one condition, then ..."

"What's that?"

"You keep it in your room."

Hannah gave a shout of joy and ran to get the carpet. Her father smiled and went to help.

***

The night was blustery. In the middle of the English Channel was a small white yacht, the Suzette, *and standing on deck with his black cloak billowing was Philippe Fontaine. He was looking at the stars through his telescope, pausing every now and then to scribble something in his notebook. But what was that? A small dark shape was moving slowly but steadily across the heavens: the magic carpet! Aboard it was a girl sitting cross-legged, with her hair streaming in the wind and a tartan blanket wrapped around her shoulders.*

"Bon voyage!" shouted Philippe Fontaine.

But she was too far off to hear him. He watched until the carpet was just a small dark speck among the stars.

Then he chuckled to himself and resumed his inspection of the heavens.

Meanwhile, back in Hannah's bedroom, the curtains billowed in through the open window and a piece of paper fluttered off the desk onto the floor. It was a note. It said:

Gone to the Taj Mahal.

Back for breakfast.

Hannah